P9-CEM-524

JUST FOR BOYS

Written by Matt Crossick
Illustrated by Rob Davis

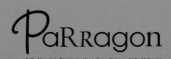

PaRragon

Bath. New York. Singapore. Hong Kong. Cologne. Delhi. Melbourne

This edition published by Parragon in 2009
Parragon
Queen Street House
4 Queen Street
Bath BA1 1HE, UK

Copyright © Parragon Books Ltd 2008

All rights reserved. No part of this publication may be reproduced, stored
in a retrieval system or transmitted, in any form or by any means, electronic,
mechanical, photocopying, recording or otherwise, without the prior permission
of the copyright holder.

ISBN 978-1-4075-1570-0

Printed in China

CONTENTS

HELP! Everything's changing!

Have you ever turned up to school wearing clothes that are two sizes too small or had a distant relative say, "My! Haven't you grown?"

Of course you have. That's because all children grow, all the time, right up until they're ... well, grown up! You grow in your sleep. You grow when you're walking around. In fact, you've grown a little since you started reading this sentence.

What's next?

When you get to a certain age, normally in your early teens, you'll notice some funny things happening. You might have even noticed some strange things starting already. Hair may be sprouting up where you didn't have any before. Your voice may be getting croaky and deep. Pimples may be appearing on your skin. There are tons of examples. So many examples, in fact, that you might need a guide book to tell you what's going on. A bit like an instruction manual for your body. And that's EXACTLY what this book is.

Food for your brain!

Read this book from cover to cover, or just dip into it when you feel like you're freaking out. It's packed full of explanations, diagrams, advice, and real-life stories. Some of it's embarrassing. Some of it's funny. A little of it is scary. But when you've finished reading, you should have a good idea of what to expect, and an understanding of what's happening to you, and some top tips on avoiding embarrassing situations.

You might just look at the chapters that interest you for now and then leave it on your shelf until you have more questions about the rest of the book.

Remember to speak to a trusted adult about anything that doesn't make sense or is different from your experience.

Throughout this book you'll see the following symbols crop up. Here's what they mean:

Readers' stories — Real-life stories!

Top tip — Advice from the experts!

Fact file — The technical stuff!

Why me?
Why now?
What's happening?

Want to know what's REALLY going on inside that body of yours? Then shut your bedroom door, put your feet up and prepare to find out ALL the answers . . .

Why me?

You don't have to be a biology expert or a super-sleuth to notice that men are different from boys. They're bigger, for a start. And they've got deeper voices. And they're COVERED in hair, all over their bodies.

But boys don't just go to bed one night and wake up the next day with manly, hairy bodies and deep voices. The process of turning from a boy into a man takes years, and it even has a special name: puberty. It normally starts in a boy's early teens. And you can bet that at the end of the process, you'll be bigger, stronger and, much hairier than you are now.

Puberty happens to different people at different times. Some boys might need to start shaving when they're only 11 or 12 years old. Other boys won't need to shave until they're 18. You never know when puberty's going to start—it just does, without any warning. But don't worry if you're way ahead of your friends, or way behind them.

How does my body know when to start changing?

Your body starts changing thanks to special chemicals called hormones, which start affecting the way your body grows in your early teens. Hormones make you grow faster, they make you hairier—they even make you notice girls more. But they can also make you emotional, insecure, and sometimes even a little paranoid. If you feel like this for no reason, don't worry—it's just your hormones acting up.

✔ Fact file

There are lots of different kinds of hormones in your body, and each one controls a different thing. For example, a hormone called melatonin regulates how much you sleep. One of the most important hormones during puberty is testosterone. It makes you more muscular, hairier, and makes your voice deeper too.

The beginning

You can't make testosterone until your brain gives the right signal to your body. One night, when you're fast asleep, you will start to make a hormone called GnRH. This happens within your brain. Once enough GnRH has been made, a part of your brain called the pituitary gland is stimulated to produce two other hormones. These travel in your blood stream and send a message to your testicles.

When your testicles have received this message, they will start to make sex hormones and sperm. Male sex hormones are called androgens; testosterone is one of these.

Androgens give instructions to parts of the body. They tell your bones to grow, your voice to crack, etc. They can also affect your moods, making you feel depressed for no apparent reason.

Male or female?

Girls can make small amounts of testosterone, and boys make some female sex hormones too.

How can I avoid puberty?

Unfortunately, puberty isn't voluntary. You can't choose when it happens, or take a break from it for a weekend. And what's worse, some parts of puberty can be pretty embarrassing.

For example, if you shoot up four inches in a year before anyone else in your class, you might feel a little awkward hanging round with your friends. And when your voice changes, you'll sound a little squeaky before you get a booming man's voice.

You'll get pimples, and you can start smelling too if you don't shower every day. In fact, there are hundreds of ways to embarrass yourself while you're going through puberty. And unless you're literally the COOLEST PERSON IN THE WHOLE WORLD, you're going to find yourself blushing and wishing the ground would swallow you up at one time or another.

I wouldn't mind so much if I wasn't so confused. Does everyone else feel like this?

Everyone will go through the same thing. And if you follow the top tips in this book, you should keep any embarrassing incidents to the absolute minimum!

You can bet that if you feel a little confused when your voice starts to sound different or you start getting hairier, everyone else will too. You might feel uncomfortable talking to your friends about it, but everyone feels confused when they go through puberty, and everyone gets embarrassed by their body changing.

Growing up can make you feel . . .

grumpy... happy... excited... angry... shy... confident... anxious... lonely... on top of the world... embarrassed... argumentative... restless... tired...

Questions, questions, I need some help!

With all these changes, you might feel you have tons of questions and no-one to ask. Remember, your parents or teachers can answer lots of them. But reading this book is a start. Read on to find out the answers to all these, and more …

- My voice sounds weird! Have I got an infection? When will it get better?

- Why haven't I started shaving yet? Everyone else in my class has!

- I'm shorter than everyone in my class! When will I catch up?

- Why am I covered in pimples? How can I get rid of them?

- My armpits REEK. What can I do?

- I think I like a girl in my class. Will my friends make fun of me?

- How can I cope with peer pressure?

- Should I really have such hairy legs?

- My mom won't let me out on my own. How can I convince her I'm growing up?

- I want to STOP growing—I feel like a freak!

Who can I talk to?

If you can't find the answer to your question in this book, don't panic. There are tons of people around who can give you advice. We recommend dads as a good place to start, after all, they went through puberty once too. Your teachers at school can give you advice too. If you think that there may be something wrong with you, have a quiet chat with your doctor or school nurse. And it's worth asking your friends if they're going through the same thing, too—though take their advice with a pinch of salt.

I... erm...

Doctor

⭐ Top tip

You'll notice other boys your age changing and going through puberty at roughly the same time as you. Be careful you don't make fun of them when they embarrass themselves. After all, it could be your turn next!

The facts about your body...

This section is about the physical changes you will go through. Ready?
Then turn the page and start learning the facts...

Taller and stronger

One of the first things people notice about puberty is a fast growth spurt. One day you'll be lounging around your house in a kid-size T-shirt; six months later you'll find yourself trying to squeeze into your dad's hand-me-downs and wearing shoes the size of small boats.

How did that happen?

Well, it's your hormones at work again. Remember, puberty is all about turning into a man. And that involves becoming man-sized, too. Over the course of a few years, you'll grow faster than you've ever grown before.

Getting bigger and stronger may sound like a pretty good deal, but it can cause problems, too. Firstly, you will find yourself needing a lot of new clothes (you might look a little silly in the tiny sweatshirt that fitted you perfectly at the beginning of the school year). Also, your brain takes a few years to work out the fact that it has a new, taller body to control— which means you can be very clumsy while you're growing.

✔ Fact file

During your growth spurt you could grow at a rate of up to 5 inches a year. In fact, 20% of your total adult height will be added during puberty. Your body knows when to stop growing when special "growth plates" on your bones fuse together. You won't notice this happen—but it occurs at the end of puberty, and means you have reached your full adult height.

Because everyone starts puberty at different times, you could find yourself growing much faster than your friends. But remember they'll be catching you up before long. So don't treat them too badly!

17

When I was fifteen years old, everyone in my class had already started their growth spurts. But I was only an inch taller than when I was eleven! All my buddies made fun of me constantly.

Just when I thought it couldn't get any worse, I finally started to grow.

I ended up growing taller than anyone else in my class—I'm six feet tall, and a star of my sports team, and no-one makes fun of me anymore!

Ryan, Boston

Don't ever... use your new strength to bully people. No-one likes a bully—plus, the small kid in your class could end up taller than you when he's been through puberty too!

Hair, hair, everywhere!

Until you're in your early teens, hair is pretty simple. It sits on your head. You put gel in it to make it look cool. But your hair is greedy. Like weeds in the garden, it's not happy just growing in one place. So it starts to creep to other areas of your body too.

Seeing hair growing on your body is an odd experience. You'll notice your friends start to get hairy, too. But you won't all grow hair at the same time.

The first place you'll see hair growing is around your penis and testicles—this is called pubic hair. To start with, it's quite thin and only grows in a small patch. After about a year it gets thicker, curlier and spreads outwards. And that's not all. Before long, you'll find your armpits getting hairy, too. And sometimes your chest and legs. And your face. In fact, almost every part of your body can get hairy as you get older.

19

How hairy will I end up?

You've probably noticed that some men are hairier than others. Some men have no chest hair at all, while some have hair all over their chests, backs, and shoulders. If you want to know how hairy you're going to get, then try having a look at your dad. These things run in the family—so if your dad is really hairy, you should think about buying yourself a razor!

Smooth: Some men only grow pubic hair and armpit hair, and the rest of their bodies stay smooth.

Medium: Most men have some chest hair and hairy legs, too.

Super hairy: And some men have hair all over their bodies!

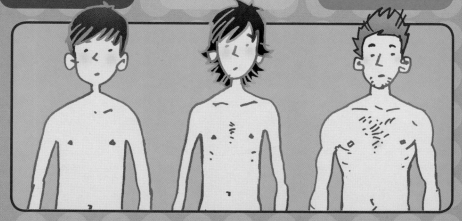

20

✅ Fact file

Hair has all sorts of functions, which is why you grow more of it as you go through puberty. It helps keep the sun off your skin; it retains your distinctive smell and it can protect parts of your body too, which is why you have pubic hair and hair on your head. The thin hair you have on your chest and the rest of your body is a leftover from our prehistoric ancestors, though, who needed it to keep warm.

⭐ Top tip

It's best not to shave your body hair, as it can itch when it grows back. Most people think body hair looks manly, anyway!

Shaving

Some people see their new, hairy faces as the perfect opportunity to grow a big bushy beard and a huge moustache. As this isn't a great look when you're at school, though, we recommend that you do what most people do, and start shaving.

The first hair on your face will be on your upper lip, and around your sideburns. You can start shaving whenever you think you need to—you don't have to wait until you've got a face full of hair to begin. But once you've started, there's no going back! Shaving makes your hair grow back thicker and faster—so before long you'll have to do it every day.

There are two types of shaving—called wet and dry. Dry shaving is where you use an electric razor, and you don't need to wash your face first. You just rub the electric razor over it like a mini lawnmower. It's very quick and easy. Wet shaving uses a traditional razor, shaving cream, and a sink full of hot water. Both methods work well—but you might find using an electric razor easier to begin with, as you can't cut yourself so easily.

If you do decide to wet shave, follow these steps to avoid looking like you've been in a nasty sword fight:

○ Wash your face in the hottest water you can take. This loosens up the hair.

○ Cover your face in shaving cream. Don't hold back!

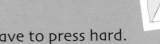

○ Shave slowly, moving the razor down your face in smooth strokes.

○ You don't have to press hard.

○ When you're done, wash your face again in cold water.

○ Repeat the steps above for any parts you've missed!

○ Splash on a little bit of aftershave, or some of your sister's moisturizer.

○ If you've cut yourself, rinse the cut and dab it dry with a tissue.

○ If you've got a face full of little cuts, consider buying an electric razor!

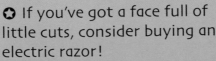

When you shave, you are cutting the hairs on your face back to the surface of your skin. Shaving cream helps when you wet shave by moisturizing your skin and making the hairs swell up, so they're easier for the razor to cut. It also stops you scraping your skin with the blade, giving you "razor burn"—where your skin gets red and itchy after shaving.

It's not very painful if you cut yourself while shaving. If you cut yourself, press a tissue on the cut to stop it bleeding.

If you have any hairs growing from moles on your face, it's better to cut them with fine scissors, rather than shaving them, as they are more likely to bleed.

⭐ Top tip

Ask your dad to show you how to shave. It's much easier if someone demonstrates!

Getting hairy can be one of the most embarrassing parts of going through puberty. But everyone goes through it—just read some of these real-life hair nightmares!

Readers' stories

I was the first kid in my class to get pubic hair. I know this, because in the showers at school everyone started pointing and staring at me! I was so embarrassed, I wouldn't get in the shower again for the rest of the school year. I only started again when the girl I sat next to in the next class complained about the smell!

James, Seattle

I first got pubic hair when I was about 11, and I didn't want my friends to make fun of me when we went swimming. So I borrowed my dad's razor, and shaved it off one morning before school. BAD IDEA! Not only did it sting, when it grew back it was really itchy. Spending the whole week with my hands down my pants scratching was more embarrassing than just turning up at the swimming pool in the first place!

Owen, New York

Down there . . .

One place where you'll notice some changes happening is between your legs. It's important to learn about these changes, because when these first happen they can be embarrassing, strange, and a little scary, too.

Around the time you start noticing your pubic hair growing, you'll also notice that your penis and testicles get bigger, and they'll change shape a little bit. This is perfectly normal, and just part of the general body changes that are going on.

Behind the scenes, though, there are more changes at work. Your testicles will start to produce sperm. And your penis will start to get hard and point upwards from time to time—this is called an erection. But let's start with the basics first. On the next page is a diagram of a penis, with all the behind-the-scenes stuff marked on it.

✅ Fact file

If you looked at a drop of sperm under a strong microscope, you would see millions of tiny tadpole-like things swimming around. Sperm cells need to be able to swim, because they have to seek out an egg to fertilize it.

Bladder—this is where urine is held until you go to the bathroom

Urethra—this is the tube through which urine and semen pass out of your penis

Foreskin—this is the loose skin at the end of an uncircumcised penis

Testicles—these produce sperm

Glans—this is the thick, sensitive part at the end of your penis

Scrotum—this is the loose skin that covers your testicles

Why are my testicles on the outside, when all my other organs are on the inside?

It's because your testicles work best when they're a little bit cooler than your body temperature. By hanging down outside, they don't get so hot, and can produce sperm more easily.

Embarrassing moments

The reason you start getting erections and producing sperm is all about reproduction. Sperm are necessary to fertilize a woman's egg. When sperm comes out of a man's erect penis, it is called ejaculation.

When you first get an erection, it can be very surprising. As you go through puberty, you'll notice you get them very often—probably every day. They will go away on their own after a few minutes, and most of the time you can just ignore them.

You'll probably also find that you get erections randomly—when you're sitting in the classroom, or walking down the street. This is just your body getting used to its new powers—but it can be embarrassing!

✅ Fact file

Your penis becomes hard during an erection thanks to the special erectile tissue inside it. This special tissue expands and gets stiffer when it is filled with blood. When you get an erection, your body is pumping blood into your penis, which makes the erectile tissue bigger and firmer. When the blood drains away again, your erection disappears.

What can I do to hide it?

✪ Wear baggy jeans or pants. They'll make any uncontrollable erections much harder to spot!

✪ Wear swimming shorts, not tight trunks. They'll be much less obvious.

✪ Think about something else while you have an erection. It will go away in a minute or two if you ignore it.

✪ Remember: not everyone is staring at you all the time. People are very unlikely to notice anything is amiss!

Big, booming voices... and how to get one!

When people talk about your voice cracking, they don't actually mean it's going to stop working! They mean that it has begun to change into a man's voice. And while it would be great (though a bit weird) if you could just wake up one morning with your new, deep voice, in reality it can take a year or two to get there.

During this time, your voice will probably go a little croaky. It will start to get deeper, but you won't be able to control it—sometimes it will be a low rumble, and sometimes you'll sound all squeaky—often during the same sentence!

Being unable to control your voice properly can be really annoying. But it will gradually get better, until you're just left with the deep parts, not the croaky high parts!

eeeek !

✅ Fact file

Everyone has a voice box (also called a larynx) in their throat—it's what allows you to speak and make different sounds. When boys go through puberty, their larynx gets much larger, and becomes visible as a lump in their throat. This lump is called your "Adam's apple", and your bigger larynx gives you a deeper voice. Girls larynxes are smaller and they don't have Adam's apples, so they have higher voices.

Readers' stories

I once had to talk in front of my whole school during assembly. Unfortunately, my voice had started cracking and on the day, my nerves made my squeaky, unpredictable voice even worse. I ended up alternately bellowing and squealing my whole speech, and the whole school cracked up before I finished.

Rob, San Diego

From the neck up

Girls have it way easier than boys in the skin department. When they get pimples, they can reach for their make-up bag and start covering them up with weird tubes of skin-colored creams. But when you're a boy, wearing make-up isn't a great way to stop people from making fun of your face.

What is acne?

Acne looks like extremely bad pimples, covering your face and sometimes your neck too. It's actually an infection of your skin pores, and is very common among teenagers. If you think you might have acne, then go and see your doctor—they can give you special creams and pills that help keep acne under control.

So here are some top tips on how to keep the annoying zit infestations to a bare minimum:

✪ Watch what you eat. Pimples are made worse by eating fatty food such as chocolate, chips, pizza, and burgers.

✪ Eat lots of fruit. Vitamins can help keep your skin clear.

✪ Drink tons of water. You'll spend more time in the bathroom, but less time in front of the mirror despairing about your skin.

✪ Don't squeeze those pimples! You could leave scars on your face that don't go away.

✪ Wash your face twice a day with a special skin-clearing soap or face wash. You can get these at your local drugstore.

✪ Do lots of exercise. A daily jog keeps your skin healthy, too.

✪ Get your beauty sleep. A good eight hour snooze can do wonders for your complexion.

✪ If your pimples are really bad, see a doctor. You might have acne, and you can get help clearing this up.

✪ Stop looking in the mirror. Your skin is never as bad as you think it is!

✓ Fact file

Your skin naturally produces and secretes an oily substance called sebum. It keeps your skin moist, waterproofs it, and stops it from cracking and becoming hard. But when you're a teenager, you produce more of this oily substance than usual, and it can end up blocking the pores that allow your skin to breathe. These blockages can lead to infections in your pores and pimples on your skin. Have a look at this
cross-section to see how a pimple is formed:

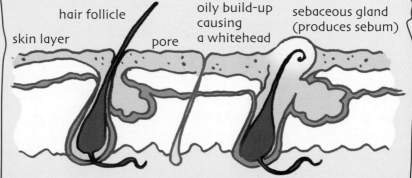

hair follicle   oily build-up causing a whitehead   sebaceous gland (produces sebum)

skin layer   pore

⭐ Top tip

Try not to get too stressed about pimples. You may think they're huge, but most people will hardly notice what state your skin is in!

Keeping clean

Being smelly is never a great idea, and once you start going through puberty, it's something you'll need to think about. Because another side-effect of all those hormones pumping around your body is a rather strong whiff.

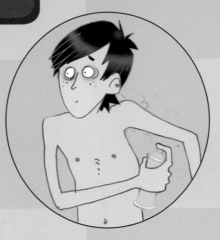

When you're young, you can spend all day running around, dry the sweat off and still smell fine the next morning. When you're in your teens, though, you can't get away with a shower every three days. You'll find you can be a little smelly when you get up in the morning, let alone after doing some exercise. So it's important to shower every day and after doing sports. And remember to use soap or shower gel, too!

Body odor

Washing isn't just about getting rid of bad smells. Bacteria thrive in warm, dark, and hairy places so be sure to wash under your arms and around your genitals regularly.

After you wash, you can use deodorants which kill the bacteria that make the smells; or you can use anti-perspirants—which control how much you sweat. Many deodorants contain anti-perspirants and can be applied using a spray can, stick, or roll-on.

Bacteria live in your clothes as well as your skin so it's important to wash them regularly. Also remember to change your underwear each day.

What is B.O.?

B.O. stands for body odor, and it refers to the smell people give off when they're hot and sweaty, or if they haven't showered recently. The smell isn't actually caused by the body itself; it's caused by millions of tiny bacteria that feed on human sweat. That's why areas of your body that get sweaty seem to smell the most—like your armpits, for example. Washing regularly gets rid of these bacteria and will keep you smelling fresh.

✔ **Fact file**

Body odor isn't just an annoying side-effect of going through puberty. In the animal kingdom, body odor is a way for animals to identify each other and find each other from a distance. It can also help male animals attract a mate— though it tends to have the opposite effect in humans in this day and age!

Sleeping in

It's a little-known fact that most of your growing is done while you're asleep. And that's one of the reasons why teenagers need much more sleep than children and adults. If you find you just can't get up in the morning, though, here is a list of a few things you can do to give yourself more energy:

⭐ Go to bed and get up at the same time every day.

⭐ Get at least eight hours sleep a night.

⭐ Eat healthy food to give you energy.

⭐ Make sure you get lots of exercise.

✔ Fact file

Because sleep is an essential human function, not having enough can have negative effects on your health. For example, your immune system can become weaker, your concentration span shorter, and your ability to absorb food can be damaged by lack of sleep. So make sure you get your eight hours a night!

Health and fitness

Look after your body. it's the only one you've got!

If you read and follow the tips on exercise and eating well in this chapter, your body will be stronger, healthier, and better looking too!

Taking care of your body

As your body gets bigger, stronger, and older, you need to start taking more care of it, too. The occasional jog in the park isn't going to be enough to keep you fit and strong, and forcing down a little salad now and then isn't going to stop you from getting overweight.

This is where eating well and exercising come in. If you want to look and feel your best, you need to think about both things every day—even if you do sneak in the occasional chocolate bar now and then! And if you find good foods that you like, and get involved in sports that you really enjoy, staying healthy can be fun rather than a drag.

Why is exercise important?

Exercise is important for a number of reasons. Firstly, it keeps you fit, so you don't get all red-faced and sweaty every time you run for a bus. It also does a lot of good behind-the-scenes, like keeping your heart and lungs healthy. And it makes you look better, too—you'll stay slimmer, get bigger muscles, and have fewer pimples if you exercise regularly. So it really is worth digging out those sneakers!

✔ Fact file

The human body evolved millions of years ago when people spent their time hunting, farming, and traveling around. It is made for running, jumping, and action—not sitting at desks or lounging on sofas. That's why we need to work at keeping our bodies fit and strong—because we don't have the natural all-day exercise that our ancestors had!

Eating healthy food is just as important as getting regular exercise if you want to stay fit. If you eat lots of junk food like burgers and pizzas, you'll put on weight, and it can make your pimples worse too. Fatty food is also bad for your heart, and can lead to diseases when you get older.

★ Top tip

Eating well doesn't mean never having a pizza or some chips. It means eating healthily most of the time—but allowing yourself a few treats, too! Read on for some healthy eating tips later in this chapter.

Bulging biceps and staying in shape

Because you're growing so fast during puberty, you can end up with quite a different shaped body to the one you began with. You might get very tall and skinny, for example. Or you might find that you put on a lot of weight and start getting fat. Either way, it's important to look after your body as much as possible—and not just to make yourself look good, either. There are tons of health benefits to staying fit—from more energy to better looks!

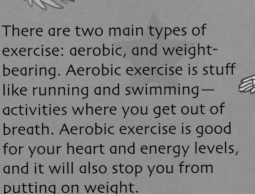

There are two main types of exercise: aerobic, and weight-bearing. Aerobic exercise is stuff like running and swimming—activities where you get out of breath. Aerobic exercise is good for your heart and energy levels, and it will also stop you from putting on weight.

42

Weight-bearing exercise involves things like push-ups, chin-ups and lifting weights. It makes you stronger and is good for your muscles. But before you run down to the gym be very careful. Doing exercises with weights before you have stopped growing can damage your joints and even stunt your growth—so only grab those dumb-bells if you are getting some expert advice on how to train. It's best to stick with exercises like push-ups that use your own body weight for now if you want to get those biceps bulging!

How much exercise should I do?

You should try to do a minimum of 20 minutes aerobic exercise at least three times a week. This is the minimum though. You should try and do something active every day if you want to stay really fit. You should also do some strength exercises once or twice a week to keep your body strong.

 **Fact file**

Aerobic fitness is all about your heart and lungs. Your lungs feed oxygen into your blood, and your heart pumps it around your body, getting essential oxygen to your muscles. When you exercise, your muscles work harder and faster and they need more oxygen. Your heart and lungs then work faster to supply it. This is why exercise makes your heart stronger, helping to prevent heart problems when you're older.

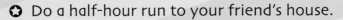

Here are some suggestions of exercises you can do:

- Go for a half-hour swim.
- Do a half-hour run to your friend's house.
- Do 25 push-ups and 25 sit-ups before you shower every morning.
- Take up a new sport at school
- Walk to the stores on a Saturday, instead of getting the bus.
- Fun stuff like skateboarding or trampolining counts as exercise, too!

Quick workout

Try doing this quick workout two or three times a week, perhaps after some aerobic exercise like a run or a swim. Do all the exercises one after the other, until you've done each exercise three times. If you aren't out of breath and sweaty at the end of it, you aren't working hard enough!

✪ Push-ups
These are great for your chest and arms. Lie face down on the floor, with your stomach muscles flexed. Slowly push yourself up with your arms. Keep your legs straight.

✪ Sit-ups
Lie on your back, with your knees bent. Put your hands behind your head, and using your stomach muscles only, curl yourself up towards your knees. Be careful not to strain your back.

More exercises over the page!

✪ Lunges

Stand straight with your hands on your hips. Then take a big step forwards, keeping your back foot where it is and bending your knees. Use your front leg to push yourself up again before repeating with the other leg.

✪ Chin-ups

You'll need a bar to do these. Keep your hands shoulder-width apart, and grip the bar firmly. Slowly pull yourself up until your chin is level with the bar. Great for your back and arms.

✪ Step-ups

Find a low step to do these on. Quickly step each foot up and down in turn, over and over again.

⭐ Top tip

Don't worry if you can't manage many push-ups or chin-ups at first. It will take a while to build up your strength. Just do as many as you can.

Always warm up with some aerobic exercise before you start your workout. And do some stretches afterwards to avoid getting an injury. Ask your gym teacher if you need some advice!

The workout

Step 1: Do 30 quick step-ups
Step 2: Do 15 push-ups
Step 3: Do 10 lunges on each leg
Step 4: Do 10 chin-ups
Step 5: Do 10 sit-ups

Repeat this set of exercises at least three times, and you've done a workout! Do it a couple of times a week, and those muscles will be bulging in no time!

Eating and drinking

Eating well affects your body in hundreds of ways, and it's not just about controlling your weight. Eating the right foods can give you more energy, too, and can make you better at sports and exercise. Your diet can also affect your immune system, so you get sick less often; it can guard you against diseases later in life; and it can help your skin look better and clearer. Professional athletes know how important a good diet is—they eat lots of pasta and protein, and no fatty foods at all, to give them an extra boost.

All that growing you're doing needs fuel. And the body's fuel is all of the breakfasts, lunches, and dinners that you munch your way through every day. It's quite simple—the more growing you're doing, the more you need to eat. Which is why when you get your growth spurt during puberty, your appetite will grow just as much at the same time!

It means you'll want to eat a lot between meals, when you're at school or in the evening. And the kind of food you eat can be very important.

If you fill yourself up on candy bars and burgers, you'll stop being hungry, but you'll be damaging your body too. Fatty foods can make your pimples worse, and can lead to you growing the wrong way—outwards, instead of upwards!

What is the right weight for me?

The right weight for you depends on your age, your height, and also your "build"— whether you are stocky or naturally thin. You can normally tell if you are overweight, because you can feel the fat on your body. But if you aren't sure, your school nurse or doctor will be able to tell you. And remember, you can be too thin as well as too fat—eating enough of the right foods is just as important as not eating bad ones!

Good food

Eating healthy is all about getting a good balance of different types of food. The following pages show some of the main food groups you should eat every day. Have a look at each group, and then think about what you ate yesterday. Did you get each group in, in every meal? If not, memorize some of the foods you like, and pick them out next time your mom asks you what you'd like to eat!

Complex carbohydrates

Complex carbohydrates are like fuel for your body. They give you energy and keep you going. Professional athletes eat loads of complex carbohydrates because they are so active. Eating things like pasta and oats is a much better way of getting energy than eating sugary foods, because the energy is released more slowly and lasts longer.

Types of carbohydrate are:
pasta
brown bread
oats
potatoes
rice

✅ Fact file

Complex carbohydrates are broken down inside your body into sugars, which are released into your blood stream. This sugar is then released into your cells, and gives you energy. Eating complex carbohydrates is much better than just eating the sugar directly, because they release energy slowly and steadily throughout the day, rather than giving you an energy rush then a slump shortly afterwards.

Protein

Protein is used by your body for growth and repair. Body builders eat tons of protein to grow their big muscles—you need to eat it regularly too, to help you grow and to help your body heal itself after injuries and after doing sports. A lot of protein comes from meat and fish—but vegetarians can eat dairy products and beans and pulses to get their fair share, too.

Types of protein are:
grilled chicken
fish
beans and pulses
lean red meat

Fruit and vegetables

Fruit and vegetables are crucial for your body because they give you the vitamins and minerals that keep you healthy. Without any fruit or veggies, your body would quickly become ill. But eating at least five different portions every day will help you fend off illness, give
you extra energy, and keep you full between meals.

Types of fruit and vegetables are:
broccoli
spinach
apples
bananas
basically, anything that grows!

Whether you prefer to eat three meals a day, or prefer to snack on smaller amounts of food throughout the day, it's important to remember not to miss out on breakfast. Your body uses energy even while you're asleep and you need to replace it in the morning.

You need to remember to brush your teeth thoroughly twice a day, too. Food particles, if left in your teeth, can lead to decay.

How should I combine all of these?

A portion of any of these food groups is roughly a fist-sized helping. So a meal of a piece of chicken, some mashed potatoes, and some broccoli would contain all three groups, and would be very good for you. A meal that just contained pasta is all carbohydrates— so you would be missing out on important protein and vegetables. See? It's easy!

✔ Fact file

Different vitamins do different things in your body. For example, vitamin C helps your body heal and fight infection. Vitamin A helps you see in the dark. Vitamin B helps give you more energy. There are lots of different vitamins—and you need to eat different fruits and vegetables to get them all.

Bad food

It's not just about the good foods. If between every healthy meal you had a big burger with extra fries, you'd still get overweight and unfit. So you need to make sure you avoid eating too many of the foods on this page.

Fatty foods

Foods with a very high fat content can be very bad for your health if you eat too much of them. Eating too much fat can make you overweight, is bad for your heart, and can lead to problems like heart attacks and strokes when you are older.

Types of fatty food:
deep-fried chicken
french fries
fast food pizza
hamburgers
potato chips

Sugary foods

Eating too many sugary foods can also make you put on a lot of weight. They are also very bad for your teeth, and finally—they can make you have energy rushes, then tired spells, rather than having lots of energy all day.

Types of sugary food:
candy
cakes
desserts
carbonated drinks
ice cream
chocolate

✔ Fact file

Fatty food increases your risk of having heart problems in later life. If you have lots of fat in your blood stream from your diet, some of it can stick to the inside of your arteries (the pipes that carry your blood around your body). Less blood can flow through them, causing problems for your heart. If you eat less fatty food, you lower your risk of these problems happening to you when you're older.

Snack ideas

If you're cutting down on unhealthy snacks, you might find you get very hungry between meals. You are growing super-fast, after all, and your body needs feeding! So try out some of these more healthy snacks instead to keep you filled up until the next meal...

- ✪ an apple and a banana—good for giving you energy
- ✪ a bowl of nuts and raisins
- ✪ fruit juice instead of carbonated drinks
- ✪ peanut butter and jelly sandwich—much better for you than chocolate
- ✪ cereal bars
- ✪ cheese and crackers

⭐ Top tip

Bring some fruit to school with you in your schoolbag to munch on between classes. That way you won't get hungry and won't get tempted by the candy machine!

Girls, girls, girls!

They look different.
They talk different.
They think different!

One of the effects of puberty is that you'll start noticing the opposite sex a little more. So read on for the inside scoop on girls . . .

It's different for girls

One of the effects of puberty is that you begin to like girls more. Of course, this doesn't mean you'll wake up one morning desperate to find yourself a girlfriend. But it does mean that you'll stop finding them so annoying, and you will probably start enjoying hanging out with them and making friends with them.

You'll probably also find that you begin to find some girls and women attractive—this is what people mean when they say that they 'like' someone. You don't have to do anything about it if you do like someone though. You can be attracted to a girl long before you feel ready to have a girlfriend—it's just your body getting ready for when you're older. But it can be confusing when it happens!

Girls worry about the changes they are going through as much as you do and they share many of the same issues.

Girls don't have to shave their faces but they grow hair in other places and many of them like to remove the hair. Some shave their legs and under their arms. Other girls use waxes and creams to remove the hair.

Girls can feel pressured to look a certain way—even before they have finished growing—they may worry about their weight or their pimples or think that their breasts are too big or small.

Boys worry about their looks as well but usually less than girls. Because girls go through puberty at different times, they can often feel very self-conscious about their bodies, especially when there are boys around. So it's important not to make fun of girls about these things. After all—you don't want them laughing at you if you do something embarrassing, do you?

59

The differences

Some of the most important changes that happen to a girl take place within her body. The main changes are listed here:

- They get taller and heavier.
- They start to have periods.
- They develop breasts.
- Their hips get wider.
- They grow body hair including pubic and armpit hair.
- They start to sweat more.
- Their sex organs develop.
- Their skin and hair may get more greasy.

✔ Fact file

Girls often start puberty before boys. They often grow taller than boys for a while, but girls stop developing earlier than boys so boys soon catch up. Girls start puberty in the same way as boys—when hormones are released into the brain.

✔ **Fact file**

A lot of the changes girls experience during puberty are about having babies. They grow breasts and start having periods when they start releasing eggs once a month. Of course, these changes don't mean a girl is ready to have a baby. But they are preparing her for when she is ready, when she has grown up.

What are periods?

You might have heard the girls in your class talking about periods—you might even have learned about them in biology at school. They're one of the main changes that a girl experiences during puberty. When a girl releases an egg, the soft lining in her womb is shed through her vagina. This bleeding lasts for a few days, and happens roughly once a month for most women. During this time, girls can experience lots of aches and pains, and it can be very confusing for them when their periods first start. Many girls feel a little depressed before a period starts. This is called pre-menstrual syndrome. Not all girls get this though.

Inside a girl's brain

You might feel self-conscious about your appearance when your body is changing, but you can bet girls feel it a lot more. Lots of their changes, like growing breasts, are more obvious than yours; and they can feel more pressure to look good, too.

You might find that you get more awkward around girls when you go through puberty; and it might seem easier to make fun of them than to have a normal conversation with them. But think about the effect this could have on their feelings. Just as you might quite like a girl, but not want her to be your girlfriend, girls take a long while to be ready for a boyfriend, too. And they can be just as nervous about boys as you are about girls!

While you might suddenly feel very awkward around girls, they might find this strange— especially if you've known them for ages. Remember, they won't have changed that much, so you can still be friends with them!

You might think that bullying and peer pressure are mainly things that affect boys, but girls have to face them too—often as much or more than the boys in their class. If you think that a girl in your class is being bullied, tell a teacher—just as you would if a boy was getting the same treatment.

📖 Readers' stories

One of the girls in my class started going through puberty much earlier than the other girls—and she grew breasts when no one else had them. Me and the other boys in my class used to really make fun of her because of them. Until one day on the way home from school I found her sitting in the street crying.
I felt really guilty—especially when the following year I started to grow really fast, and I got made fun of a lot. I realized how bad it can make you feel.

Jamie, Phoenix

I bet he thinks I'm ugly!

I'm too fat!

📖 Readers' stories

I had been friends with the girl next door for years—since we were about four years old. But when I started going through puberty, I began to notice that she was really pretty. I became totally uncomfortable around her whenever she came over, whereas we used to talk for hours. It's only when I overheard her telling a friend that I was being really strange that I snapped out of it and started treating her normally again. She must still wonder why I was behaving so oddly, though!

James, Miami

Feelings, embarrassment, and how to stay happy!

Now you've learned about what goes on on the outside, find out what's going on inside . . .

Embarrassment... and how to deal with it!

If you've been reading all about the body changes that happen during puberty, you might get the impression that your teenage years are specifically designed to humiliate you. And while this is an exaggeration, you're going to face some awkward situations along the way. So here are a few points to keep the blushes at bay...

✪ Remember—any body changes you are experiencing are much more obvious to you than they are to anyone else. If you ignore them, others will too.

✪ Sometimes someone standing there with their voice cracking is funny! If it's happening to you, try making a joke out of it, rather than wishing the ground would swallow you up.

✪ Confidence is everything. If you look super-confident, no-one will think to comment about your new hairy body. If you're looking all nervous and scared, your classmates will think something is up.

✪ If you're finding that confidence is hard to build up, remember that everyone in your class will go through puberty at some point. Even the biggest bully will be feeling insecure when his voice cracks.

✪ Make sure you've done all the little things that can keep you out of embarrassing situations—like showering every day so you don't get smelly, and eating a balanced diet to help clear your pimples.

✪ Don't let the fear of something embarrassing happening to you stop you from doing things. No matter what humiliating scrapes you get yourself into, everyone will have forgotten about them within a few days.

✪ If you feel anxious or very nervous about the changes you are going through, then tell somebody. Your parents or teachers can almost certainly help you out!

⭐ Top tip

Keeping a journal can help you feel more in control of your emotions.

Friends and family

Have you ever got to the point where you are happy one moment and angry the next? This is one of the biggest changes you go through during puberty and it's to do with those hormones again.

When you are between the stages of being a boy and a man you can feel like you don't belong in either place. You're not a kid anymore but you can feel like you don't feel like taking on the responsibilities of an adult either. You want to be seen as an individual—sometimes separate from your family with your own ideas about things. At the same time, you need the support that your family and friends give you. It's easy to feel confused about what's going on around you.

Try to imagine how your family and friends are feeling. To them it may seem as if you are rejecting them—they may be hurt that you don't seem to want to spend time with them anymore.

Friends make a whole lot of difference when you're growing up. They understand what we're going through. They share our worries and listen to our problems so that we don't feel alone. They introduce us to new ideas and laugh with us. It's easy to feel that our friends are more important than anything else in our life.

Finding friends isn't always easy. You may have to move to a new town, leaving old friends behind and making a whole set of new ones. No-one likes to feel like an outsider, but it's easy to start feeling like one—especially if everyone else seems smarter or cooler than you. However, don't let appearances fool you. Remember that everyone goes through the same thing when growing up and they will have the same concerns as you.

★ Top tip

Remember that good friendships are based on give and take. Don't demand endless support if you are not prepared to give any in return. However, don't let someone make you into a doormat by telling you how to behave and what to do.

Bullying

It's no secret that boys make fun of each other all the time—and that sometimes it can be very personal and upsetting. And when you're going through puberty, you might feel especially vulnerable to bullying. Partly because your body might make you stand out from the crowd, and partly because you'll feel more sensitive to people laughing and making jokes about you. So try and be prepared with some killer comebacks if you get targeted!

⭐ Top tip

...for beating bullies

- Don't show you're upset: it's what they want you to do.
- Remember—they're the one with the problem, not you.
- Practice some of your own comebacks to use.
- Never resort to violence: it won't solve anything.
- Walk away from any bad situation.

Joking around is one thing but when it starts really upsetting you, or when it happens all the time, it becomes something else: bullying. If people's jokes or comments are really getting you down, make sure you tell your parents or a teacher, and put a stop to it at once.

Don't let your friends pressure you into doing things you don't feel are right for you. Sticking up for yourself and your own ideas are an essential part of growing up, and doing stuff you don't want to do will make you feel miserable. Below are some comebacks for beating bullies:

You're so hairy you look like a gorilla!

⭐ I'm not fat—I'm training for the football team!

⭐ Hey—I'm only hairy because I'm more manly than you!

⭐ The view's much better up here.

⭐ At least I don't sound like a baby any more!

⭐ Why should I care what you think?

Friends and peer pressure

As you grow older, it's likely that you'll get more independent, and spend more time with your friends without your parents around. While this is fun, it can also mean you can get into situations you aren't comfortable with.

For example, your friends might want to go and do something you know is wrong—like playing somewhere dangerous, or stealing something from a store. And you might find it very hard to say "no" to them, because you don't want to seem like a scaredy-cat, or because they might make fun of you if you don't go along.

When you feel you have to do something you aren't happy with like this, it's called peer pressure, and it's very common. You need to be ready to deal with it when it comes up—by being firm and persuading your friends not to do something dangerous or wrong, or by telling them you don't want to get involved. This can be very difficult to do—but it's a sign of a strong person if you can manage it. Being armed with some good excuses always helps—try some of these to get you started, and make up some more of your own so you're always ready:

✪ I can't do that—my parents will ground me for ever!

✪ I'm on the basketball team—I don't want to risk getting injured!

✪ I'm not really into that kind of thing. I'll catch up with you guys later.

⭐ Top tip

When boys are in a group together, they can feel under pressure to go along with the rest of the group, without being happy about it. If this happens to you, try to find someone else in the group who shares your view. It's much easier if there are two of you ducking out.

Family stuff

It's not just your relationship with your friends that can change when you go through puberty. How you get along with your parents can also change as you grow up.

When you're a child, your parents do everything for you, they cook your dinner, buy your clothes, drive you to a friend's house, pick you up from after school activities... but as you get older, you'll probably find you want to do more stuff on your own.

You might want to re-decorate your room, or choose your own clothes, or see your friends at the weekend instead of hanging around with your folks. And all of this can lead to arguments between you and your parents.

While you might think they are being totally unreasonable about something, try and see it from their point of view, too. Going through puberty can be hard for your mom and dad as well as you—they are watching their boy turn into a man and it will take them as much time as it takes you to adjust.

Here are some examples of the things you are most likely to argue about:

- ✪ Playing music too loud.
- ✪ Not hanging round with the family any more.
- ✪ Wanting to buy your own clothes.
- ✪ Spending too much time with friends.
- ✪ Spending too much time in your room.
- ✪ Not telling your mom where you are.
- ✪ Staying up late, and sleeping late.

Most of these arguments could be settled quite easily by meeting your parents halfway—agree to spend Sunday afternoons with the family, for example. Or agree that you'll only play your music loud before 8pm. You get some of what you want—and your mom and dad will stop yelling at you about it!

How can I get more independence?

Many of the arguments teenagers have with their parents are about one thing: independence. As you get older, you'll want to do more stuff on your own, without your mom and dad tagging along or organizing things for you. You might also want to stop doing things with them at the weekends.

The arguments generally start when your parents don't think you're ready for extra responsibility, while you think you are. For example, you might want to go to a friend's party, and come home at midnight when your parents want to come and pick you up at 9.30pm.

Arguing and shouting with your parents isn't always the best way to solve things, though. It's a much better idea to get your parents to trust you more. If they trust you, they'll be much less worried about your increasing independence.

Readers' stories

My cell phone saved me from lots of arguments with my mom and dad. I worked out that they only got angry with me because they were worried all the time—so whenever I went into town shopping with my friends, I just texted my mom to tell her I was OK. She even paid for the texts—and stopped shouting at me when I got back, too!
Andrew, Chicago

Below are a few tips on how to improve your relationship with your mom and dad:

⭐ Agree a time you'll be home with your parents, and always make sure you keep to it. If you can't get home by 9.30, they'll never let you out until 10.00.

⭐ Agree with them some 'friends time' and some "family time" so that they know you won't be spending your whole weekend out with your friends.

⭐ Always tell your parents where you are, and who you're with. They'll feel much happier letting you go off on your own if they know what you're up to.

⭐ Introduce them to your friends. They won't imagine you getting into trouble if they know how nice they are!

⭐ Call in and tell your parents that you're OK from time to time. The less they worry about you, the nicer they'll be to you!

⭐ Never lie to your mom and dad about where you're going. If they find out, all that trust will be destroyed—and you'll never get the extra independence you're after.

Feeling down?

Another result of all the hormones running round your body is that you can sometimes feel a bit "down", without really knowing why. You might not feel like going out and doing anything, you might feel tired, or feel a bit miserable—all for no apparent reason.

In fact, it's due to the chemicals in your body that control your moods. But that doesn't really help you if you're down in the dumps! The main thing is not to worry—your moods will pass, and feeling a little down doesn't mean you're "depressed" or seriously unhappy.

Of course, if these feelings don't go away, you should speak to an adult who you trust. There is help available if you need it!

✔ Fact file

There are over 50 different hormones in the body, and the balance of these hormones controls your moods as well as hundreds of other things inside you. Because your body starts producing much more of certain hormones during puberty—such as testosterone—the balance can become upset, which leads to your moods swinging without you being able to do anything about it.

If you're feeling down for a few days or more, here are a few tips for lifting yourself out of it and giving yourself an energy boost:

✪ Do some exercise. Getting fit is proven to improve your energy levels, and mood!

✪ Eat well. Eating sugary foods can make mood swings worse.

✪ Don't shut yourself away in your room. Seeing some friends will help you snap out of your mood quicker!

Don't ever suffer in silence. If you are feeling depressed or low, tell a friendly adult. There is always a way to help you out if you need it.

⭐ **Top tip**

Watch out for your friends' moods, too. If one of your friends seems a bit low for no reason, tell him it's OK—it's just his hormones working overtime!

Drugs and how to stay safe

As you spend more time with your friends and less time with your parents, you might come into contact with new people— and dangerous situations. And one of the things you need to be careful of is drugs, and people offering them to you.

There are many different types of drugs, and all of them are dangerous in different ways.

Some of these drugs are very addictive, and can ruin lives. Others can kill you right away if you react badly to them. And some can make you lose control and do things you don't want to.

The best policy if anyone offers you drugs is to say "no", firmly. Never let yourself be pressured into taking something— remember, just because it hasn't had a bad effect on someone else, doesn't mean you won't react badly to it. And the risks can be very high.

If you haven't been told about all the effects of drugs and what they do to you, then you need to find out. Ask your parents or a teacher—there should be leaflets and books in your school.

Smoking

Although you might not think of
smoking cigarettes as taking
drugs—after all, you can
buy them openly from the
convenience store—they do
in fact contain a powerful
drug called nicotine. Nicotine is
very addictive, which is why people
can't give up smoking. And smoking is
incredibly bad for your health—it can cause deadly diseases
when you're older, and will make you much less good
at sports and exercise while you're younger. So don't let
anyone pressure you into smoking that
first cigarette!

Alcohol

You have probably seen your parents drink alcohol lots of times—and as you get older, people will begin to offer it to you, too. But remember, it's illegal for kids under the age of 21 to buy alcohol or drink.

Boys are often pressured to try alcohol by someone presenting drinking as an adult thing to do. But making your own choices and saying 'no' is the best way to show how grown up you are.

⭐ Top tip

If you are worried that one of your friends is taking drugs or drinking, then go and see an adult about it right away. You are not tattling—it's helping your friend out.

Real-life problems

The last section of this book is a collection of real readers' problems, and some advice on how to deal with the issues they have faced.
If your problem isn't in here, make sure you ask someone about it.

Real-life problems . . . and what to do about them!

Q: Over the last two years, it feels like my parents are constantly yelling at me. They yell at me when I spend an afternoon in my room; they yell at me when I go out with my friends; they even yell at me for what I wear! What can I do to get them off my back?

A: Your parents are probably just trying to adjust to the new person you have become since you started going through puberty. And they might be worried about you when you go out on your own. Instead of arguing with them, try reassuring them that you're responsible and won't get into trouble—and remind them that adjusting to your new body is hard for you, too. If you both understand each other more, you should be able to get along better.

I'm not late!

It's 9.30! Where have you been?

Q: I'm very tall for my age—I'm 13, and the tallest person in my class. I wouldn't mind, but my friends (who I've known for years) constantly make fun of me over it. I know they're trying to be funny, but it really gets me down. What can I do?

A: It can be very awkward if you start puberty much earlier than your friends, and they probably feel a bit nervous about it too—which is why they make fun of you so much. If they are good friends, the best thing to do is sit down with them individually and tell them that you feel very self-conscious about your height and would rather they kept quiet about it. If they know how much it's getting you down, they should stop. And before long they'll be catching up to you—which should solve the problem!

Q: I've got a problem: I've started to really like a girl in my class. I don't want a girlfriend or anything like that, but it's made me really awkward whenever I talk to her—and I sit next to her in a couple of classes. What can I do?

A: This may sound impossible—but try and forget that you like her when you're with her, and just treat her like one of your friends. If you get used to relaxing in her company, you won't feel so shy—and she won't think you've gone all weird!

85

Q: I've got a really embarrassing problem. I've started a new school—and I seem to be the only person in my class who has started going through puberty. Anyway, I'm worried about the showers after gym, because I'm sure I'll be the only person with pubic hair and armpit hair. What can I do?

A: The shower room can be awkward when you're going through puberty—but the best thing you can do is relax and not think about it. If you look nervous and try to hide your body, you'll attract attention and comments. If you stride into the showers confidently, people are much less likely to make fun of you. If anyone says anything—just tell them it will happen to them soon, too!

Q: Help! Over the last couple of years, I have developed really bad B.O. I even get it when I haven't done any sports or exercise that day. People are starting to make jokes about it and I don't know what to do!

A: Firstly, make sure you are showering often enough—every morning before school, and after exercise. Then try using an anti-perspirant deodorant after you shower. If you find you are still smelling a little, you can always bring the deodorant with you in your school bag in case of emergencies.

Q: I'm 14 years old now, and all my friends often go into town together on a Saturday afternoon to hang out at the park. But my mom never lets me go—she says I'm too young to be going out on my own. It's really embarrassing as I have to keep saying "no" to my friends. How can I convince her that I'm not a little kid any more?

A: The key here is proving to your mom that you'll be safe if she lets you out on your own—she's probably nervous that something will happen to you or you'll get into trouble. Start by asking her if you can just go out for an hour or two—and suggest she comes and picks you up if she's worried about you getting home OK. And text her during the afternoon to tell her you are safe. If she sees that she can trust you doing this, she might gradually let you stay out for longer on your own.

Q: I've heard some of the girls in my class talking about tampons and pads. What are these? Have they got something to do with periods?

A: Yes, they are to do with girls' periods. They are both kinds of small absorbent pads that soak up the blood a girl releases during her period. They wear them so that they can carry on doing normal day-to-day activities during their period.

87

Q: My friends have recently started hanging out in our local shopping mall after school and at weekends. I go along sometimes too—but it makes me nervous, because there are normally older boys there who sometimes drink alcohol and smoke cigarettes. Should I keep going down? It's the only way I can see my friends!

A: The first thing to do is have a talk with your friends. It's possible that they don't feel comfortable with it either, and would be much happier doing something else. Try suggesting some fun stuff to do together, too, that doesn't involve hanging round with older boys. And if you do go and hang out with them—be very careful not to be pressured into anything you don't want to do. And if you feel nervous, go home right away.

Q: I have really bad skin. It's covered in pimples and I wash and scrub my face lots of times during the day but they won't go away. What can I do?

A: Washing your face can help reduce acne, but don't do it too often. If you wash your face more than three times a day or too harshly it can make your skin worse.

You can also buy creams at the drugstore to help with acne but follow the instructions carefully as some creams can be irritating if you use too much.

If you think your pimples are out of control, then talk to your parents about seeing a doctor.

Q: I didn't really worry about anything body-related until recently, when I started to get tons of hair all over my body. Most of it doesn't really matter—but my chest is getting really hairy, and it's quite embarrassing: it even pokes out the top of my T-shirt. Should I shave it off?

A: You may find your hairy chest embarrassing, especially if no-one else you know has got one yet. But shaving it off isn't a great idea. When body hair grows back, it can be very itchy. And it will grow back quickly, too, so your smooth chest won't last long. It's better to leave it be, and get used to your new hairy look!

Stuff you might hear, see or read—and what it means!

acne

Acne is a condition that affects your skin, making it very pimply and red. It is treatable, though, so if you think you might have it, go and see your doctor.

Adam's apple

This is the lump that grows in your throat when your voice cracks. It contains your new, deeper vocal chords.

bacteria

Microscopic life forms. Some are harmful to us and some are healthy.

bladder

Bag-like organ that collects urine (see also URINE).

breasts

Girls develop breasts during puberty. They are part of girls' bodies getting ready for reproduction—as breasts produce milk when a woman has a baby.

B.O.

Stands for body odor—and is a common way of referring to the smell that people give off when they sweat or don't wash for a while.

blackhead

A type of pimple, where a black dot is visible on the tip of the pimple. Caused by some dirt blocking one of the pores on your skin.

cells

The smallest units of life. All living things are made of cells. Some such as BACTERIA may have just one cell.

deodorant

Nice-smelling stuff that you can spray yourself with after you shower, to stop you smelling .You can also get deodorant you roll on to your skin, too.

ejaculation

When sperm shoots out of the end of a man's penis. This is called ejaculation.

erection

When a man becomes aroused, his penis fills with more blood than usual, and becomes hard and points upwards. This is called an erection.

gender

Your sex—whether you are male or female.

genitals

Genitals is a term that is used for the "sex organs" of both men and women. So, a man's penis and testicles, or a woman's vagina.

glans

The thick tip of a man's penis.

hormones

The chemicals in your body that cause you to grow and change shape during puberty.

mood swing
When you find you are alternately very energetic and happy, then rather glum and moody. Mood swings are a side-effect of the hormones in your body, and are perfectly normal.

ovaries
These are the organs in a woman that produce an egg every month.

peer pressure
This is a term that describes the pressure that your friends or classmates might put on you to do something you aren't comfortable with.

periods
If a woman's egg isn't fertilized, it is flushed out of her body. The soft layer that lines her womb is flushed out at the same time, leading to a discharge from her vagina. This is her period, and lasts for a few days every month.

pimple
pimple on your skin are caused by dirt and grease blocking your pores. They are most common on the face and neck, but can appear elsewhere too, like your arms and back.

pore
The tiny holes in your skin are called pores. They can get blocked up with dirt and grease to cause pimples.

puberty
This is the term that describes all of the physical changes a boy goes through to become a man—and the changes a girl goes through to become a woman.

pubic hair
Hair that grows around the external sex organs.

93

scrotum
The loose skin that surrounds your testicles.

semen
The white liquid that contains your sperm, which comes out when you ejaculate.

sperm
Tiny, tadpole-like cells that a man produces in his testicles. They come out of a man's penis in semen when a man ejaculates, and can fertilize a woman's egg to make her pregnant.

stubble
This is the short, rough hair that grows back on a man's face after he has shaved. When it gets too long, he needs to shave again.

testicles
The testicles produce sperm (see above).

testosterone
One of the main hormones insides the body that causes growth, hair to grow, and other bodily changes during puberty.

urine
Urine comes out of the same hole in your penis as sperm does, but not at the same time. Urine is stored in the bladder before coming out when you go to the toilet.

95

Index